**Robert**
**and the**
**Back-to-School**
**Special**

# Robert

## and the
## Back-to-School
## Special

### by Barbara Seuling
### Illustrated by Paul Brewer

Cricket Books
Chicago

Library of Congress Cataloging-in-Publication Data

Seuling, Barbara.
   Robert and the back-to school special / by Barbara Seuling ;
illustrations by Paul Brewer.— 1st ed.
       p. cm.
Summary: The new school year gets off to a not-so-good start
when Robert gets a bad haircut, but things improve when his
father helps him plan a party for Halloween.
   ISBN 0-8126-2662-1 (cloth : alk. paper)
   [1. Schools—Fiction. 2. Halloween—Fiction. 3. Fathers and
sons—Fiction.] I. Brewer, Paul, ill. II. Title.
   PZ7.S5135 Rm 2002
   [Fic]—dc21

                                              2002009325

To Debby Vetter, Paula Morrow, and
Tony Jacobson—a gazillion thanks!
—B. S.

For Brad Horwitz, Dave Griffith, and Da Moon.
—P. B.

# Contents

Back-to-school Special 1

First Day of School 6

Different 10

Summer Vacation 14

The Haircut 19

Lumpy and Bumpy 26

Humiliated 31

Sunset Pines 36

Seven Wonders 44

Just Ask 50

The Scariest Thing             55
Surprise Party                 61
Too Late Now                   67
Uncle Albert                   72
Vel-l-l-l-come!                78
Eyeballs and Worms             84
Scary Stories                  89
Gotcha!                        93
The Stranger                   99

# Back-to-school Special

**R**obert unbuckled his seat belt and hopped out of the car. "Come on, Paul." His best friend, Paul, jumped out right behind him.

"Wait up, guys," said Robert's mom, locking the car door. "There's no need to rush. School doesn't start until Monday."

The boys slowed down as they headed for the automatic doors. Mrs. Dorfman followed behind them.

They passed right by the mall directory. They knew exactly where they were going first—to the pet store. Robert had to buy food for Fuzzy, his pet tarantula, and a chew stick for Trudy, the class hamster. He couldn't wait to see the class pets again after a whole summer off. Brian Hoberman had taken care of Sally, the class snake (and Robert's favorite). Abby Ranko had gotten to take Trudy home. Robert hoped she had remembered to give Trudy chew sticks.

The pet shop was at the other end of the mall. Robert bought the tarantula food and the chew stick. Next was the drug-store, with its special back-to-school sale on paper and pens and other supplies.

Robert bought a fat notebook with a dog on the cover. Paul got one with a picture of a rocket being launched.

When they were finished shopping, Mrs. Dorfman asked if they were hungry.

"I'm starving," said Robert, heading for the escalator. The smells of pizza, hamburgers, fries, tacos, hot dogs, pretzels, and stuffed baked potatoes filled the air.

"Me, too," said Paul, following Robert up the last few steps to the food court.

They all had hamburgers and fries. "Did you get everything you need?" asked Mrs. Dorfman. Robert nodded as he dipped a fry into a puddle of ketchup. Paul nodded, too, his mouth full.

They left the food court and walked toward the exit. As they passed Ernesto's Hair Emporium, Mrs. Dorfman stopped.

"Robert, we should get you a haircut while we're here," Mrs. Dorfman said.

They were having a back-to-school special, too.

Oh no. Robert hated getting haircuts at the mall. The barber, Ernesto, always teased him about his curly hair. Once he said, "My daughter would love to have curls like these." Robert had wanted to slide under the chair.

"Mom, can't we wait? It's our last Saturday before school starts. Paul and I want to ride our bikes."

"You didn't tell me you were going bike riding today," said Mrs. Dorfman.

"I forgot," said Robert.

"Well, they do look pretty busy," said Mrs. Dorfman. "Maybe we can come back during the week. I wish you would tell me when you make plans."

Robert rolled his eyes in relief. Paul smiled as they headed for the exit again.

# First Day of School

The air was buzzing around him as Robert walked into the classroom. The first day of school was always exciting. It was fun to see the other kids and Mrs. Bernthal again, and the class pets, too.

He sat down at his usual place—Table Four—with Paul and Vanessa. From his seat, he could look right across at Susanne Lee Rodgers, the smartest girl in the class, at Table Three.

Mrs. Bernthal welcomed them all back to school. "Aren't we lucky to be together again?" she said. "You may take a few minutes to get reacquainted." Chairs scraped the floor as children got up and moved around.

Robert loved Mrs. Bernthal. She was always kind and cheerful, and never made anyone feel stupid. Robert remembered when she had brought Sally to school. "She's a green ribbon snake." Mrs. Bernthal had said. "This is for being the best class in the whole school."

Robert went to the back of the room where the animals were kept. There was Sally, all smooth and pretty, resting on her cedar chips and twigs as always.

"Hi, Sally," said Robert, reaching in to stroke her slim green body with his finger. She wiggled into an S-curve.

The class was still buzzing as kids said hello to each other and showed off their new sneakers or book bags.

After a while, Robert took the chew

stick out of his pocket and went over to Trudy's cage. Trudy wasn't there. Puzzled, he looked around for Abby. She was at her table, talking to Matt Blakey and Brian. Robert walked over.

"Hi, Abby," he said. "Hi, Matt. Hi, Brian."

"Hi, Robert," said Abby. The boys just grunted.

"Um, I was wondering," said Robert. "You took Trudy home over the summer vacation, didn't you?"

Abby nodded.

"Where is she?"

Abby looked down. "I'm sorry," she said in a soft little voice. "Trudy's dead."

Robert gasped. He felt as though he had been punched in the stomach. He went back to his table.

"Trudy's dead," he told Paul, sliding into his chair.

"Oh no," said Paul. He shook his head sadly. "Poor old Trudy."

Yeah. Things did not look great, and this was only the beginning of the first day of school.

# Different

Robert and Paul slid into their usual lunchroom seats. Robert opened his sandwich and began picking the salami out of it.

"You look different." It was Susanne Lee Rodgers. Robert didn't have to turn around to know that. Her voice made Robert grind his teeth.

"I'm the same," he said to her, closing up his sandwich again.

"Hmmm," said Susanne Lee. "I don't think so." She walked away to join Vanessa

Nicolini and Emily Asher. They always sat
together at lunch.

"Do I look different to you?" Robert asked
Paul.

Paul looked at him over his tomato-and-
cheese sandwich. "Uh-uh," he said.

What is Susanne Lee talking about? Robert wondered. What could be different about me?

Over at Susanne Lee's lunch table, Vanessa and Emily giggled. Robert was sure it was about him. He looked down the front of his shirt. He checked his zipper. They were both O.K.

Back in the classroom, there were more giggles. Robert excused himself and took the pass to go to the boys' room. He felt the seat of his pants. It was not torn. He checked his shoes. There was no toilet paper trailing from them. He looked in the mirror.

There was nothing gross on his face or between his teeth. He looked closely at one eye, then the other. He saw a couple of freckles on his nose he didn't remember. Could that be it? He leaned over the sink and stuck his tongue way out. It looked like his regular tongue.

The door opened, and Brian walked in. He stared at Robert.

"Hi," he said.

Robert muttered, "Hi," and hurried back to the classroom.

First Trudy and now this. Robert wished he could start the day all over again.

# Summer Vacation

After lunch, they settled down again at their tables. Mrs. Bernthal took a piece of chalk and wrote SUMMER VACATION on the chalkboard.

"Did anyone do anything special this summer?" she asked.

Joey Rizzo raised his hand. Mrs. Bernthal called on him.

"My dad took me to a baseball game at Yankee Stadium."

Mrs. Bernthal wrote BASEBALL on the chalkboard. "What can you tell us about it?" she asked.

"We had hot dogs and soda," said Joey.
"Anything else?"

Joey thought for a minute. "Oh," he said. "Yeah. And peanuts."

"Very nice, Joey," said Mrs. Bernthal.
Susanne Lee raised her hand.

"Yes, Susanne Lee. Tell us what you did on your summer vacation."

"I went to the American Museum of Natural History in New York City," she said. "One dinosaur skeleton is so big it takes up almost the whole room."

Mrs. Bernthal added MUSEUMS to the list.

"We'll be taking a class trip to the museum next month," she said. "There's a special Egypt exhibit, with mummies."

That would be fun! Robert had never seen a mummy.

Abby raised her hand.

"Abby, tell us about your summer vacation," said Mrs. Bernthal.

Abby got up slowly. "I want to tell you about Trudy," she said in a tiny voice. The class got very quiet.

"One day I went to feed her," she said, "and she wasn't moving. I was scared. I called my mom. My mom looked at Trudy and said she was dead." Abby sniffled a little as she spoke.

"I cried. I told my mom I fed her and gave her water every day and cleaned her cage once a week. She said Trudy probably just died of old age. I cried anyway. I was afraid no one in the class would like me anymore. They would think I killed Trudy."

Robert felt a lump in his throat. He *had* been a little mad at Abby when he found out about Trudy. Now he felt sorry for her. It could have happened to anyone, even him. He imagined how terrible he would feel if Trudy had died while he was taking care of her.

Abby sat down. Robert saw Pamela Rose lean over to Abby and whisper something.

Emily Asher was next, talking about her family's trip to visit relatives in North Carolina.

Later, they got into groups to work on math. Robert was in the same group as Abby.

"You were a very good hamster monitor," he told her. "And everyone still likes you." He went back to his math problem. Then he said, "What did you do with her?"

"We buried her in the backyard," Abby said. "In a cookie box."

Robert smiled. "That's nice," he said. "Trudy loved cookies."

Abby smiled for the first time that day.

# The Haircut

When the bell rang, Robert and Paul grabbed their book bags and jackets and left together. Giggles came from behind them. It was Susanne Lee and Emily. What was so funny? Paul just shrugged, but Robert was really bothered by it.

They walked to Robert's house to do their homework. Suddenly, Robert realized what the problem must be. His hair! His mother had told him he needed a haircut. Why hadn't he listened? He opened the front door with his key. Nobody else was home yet. They went upstairs to Robert's room.

"You've got to do me a big favor," he said to Paul.

Paul sat in the beanbag chair they used for all their important thinking. "Sure. What?"

"I need you to cut my hair," said Robert.

"No way!" said Paul, jumping up. "I don't know how to cut hair!"

"You've got to. It's a matter of life and death, almost. I won't go back to school tomorrow unless my hair is cut. Everyone is laughing at me. If I tell my mom, she'll make me go to Ernesto's. You've got to help me. You're my best friend."

Robert opened his desk drawer and took out a pair of scissors. He held them out to Paul.

Paul took the scissors from Robert. He looked miserable. Reluctantly, he started snipping. He snipped there, he snipped here. *Snip, snip, snip.* Robert was getting more fidgety every moment. Finally, he couldn't stand the suspense any longer.

"Well? What's happening? How does it look?"

"I—I don't know," said Paul.

Uh-oh. That didn't sound good.

Robert jumped up and ran to the bathroom mirror. His hair looked like a lunar landscape. Bumps. Holes. Uneven.

"Oh no!" he cried.

"I told you I didn't know how to do this!" Robert saw that Paul was really upset.

The door downstairs slammed. That must be his brother, Charlie. Robert tried not to panic.

"It's fine," he told Paul, even though it wasn't.

"Really?" said Paul.

Robert felt his head. He gulped. "Sure. It's not so bad."

Paul packed up his things. "I have to go," he said.

"I'm sorry, Paul," said Robert. "I shouldn't have asked you to cut my hair."

"It's O.K," said Paul.

After Paul left, Robert had to think fast.

His dad would be home soon. Feeling desperate, Robert went to Charlie's room. Although Charlie sometimes teased him, once in a while he was O.K.

"What's up?" asked Charlie, his earphones hanging around his neck.

"Can you help me?" asked Robert.

Charlie looked up and laughed. "What happened to you?"

"It's not important. I just need you to fix it for me. Can you?"

Charlie stared at Robert. "Fix it? You want me to fix that mess?"

Robert gulped. "Yeah."

Charlie hesitated. "O.K. Sure." He grinned. "Come over here and sit down." Robert did as he was told.

Charlie fished around on his desk for a pair of scissors. "This should be easy," he said. He started clipping. Robert saw chunks of hair falling to the floor.

"Not too short!" he said.

"The only way to fix this is to get it real short, like mine," said Charlie. "Hold still."

Charlie had a buzz cut. Robert hated buzz cuts. He ran away before one more chunk of hair fell.

"What're you doing?" cried Charlie.

In the bathroom, Robert looked in the mirror and groaned. The hair on one side of his head was much shorter than the hair on the other.

"What am I going to do?" he said. If Susanne Lee thought he looked different before, what would she think now?

He ran to his room, closed the door, and locked it. He would just stay in there until his hair grew out.

# Lumpy and Bumpy

"**R**obert, I'm not going to call you again. Come down to dinner NOW."

Robert's parents had been coaxing him to come downstairs to eat dinner for half an hour. This time he heard his dad's "no more nonsense" voice. Robert had held out as long as he could. He would have to go downstairs to eat dinner with his family.

*Thump, thump, thump.* He thumped down the stairs in his sneakers and slid into his seat at the table. He wore the over-the-head rubber monster mask his dad had given him last Halloween.

"Robert, what on earth is that?" cried his mother.

"It's my Halloween mask," said Robert. It sounded more like "Im eye allowee mack."

"Take that thing off, Robert," his father ordered.

"I have to get used to it for Halloween," said Robert. It sounded like "I happto getchooz tootfor allowee."

"Halloween is still a long way off," said his father.

"Yes, Robert. Take it off. It's not healthy. You'll smother. Besides, you won't be able to eat your dinner." Mrs. Dorfman piled spaghetti onto Robert's plate.

Charlie jumped in. "It has holes for breathing," he said. "You can suck spaghetti right through the mouth hole. Show them, Robert." He lifted a strand of spaghetti off Robert's plate and stuck it through the mouth hole. With a long *shluuuuuuuuurrrrrp*, the spaghetti disappeared.

It was good to have Charlie sticking up
for him. Of course, Charlie was probably
just protecting himself. After all, Charlie
had played a part in this haircut disaster.

"That's it, Robert," said Mr. Dorfman firmly. "Remove that thing at once."

Slowly, Robert removed the mask. Mr. Dorfman's mouth fell open. Mrs. Dorfman let out a high-pitched squeak. Charlie couldn't help himself. He roared with laughter.

"I think we need an explanation," said Mr. Dorfman. The vein in his neck was throbbing.

Robert cleared his throat. "Everyone was laughing at me," he said. "I had to do something."

"Why would they laugh at you?" asked his mother, stifling her own laughter.

"I thought it was probably my hair," he said.

"What was wrong with your hair?" said his father, who was beginning to laugh, too.

"It looked funny." Robert stared at the mound of spaghetti in front of him.

Usually, he loved spaghetti, but now it might just as well be a plate full of worms.

"It did not look funny, Robert. It was just a little long. I knew we should have seen Ernesto on Saturday." His mom tried to reassure him, but soon everyone was laughing.

"You can't go to school like that," his mother continued. "Your hair is lumpy and bumpy. You look . . ."

"Deranged?" offered Charlie.

"No. That's not what I was going to say. You look . . . well . . . sort of . . . unfinished. And Ernesto's is closed now. I'll have to fix it myself. I'm sure I can get it to look a little better than it does now."

Great. Just what Robert needed. Another person taking a pair of scissors to his hair.

# Humiliated

In the morning, Robert searched his closet for a hat he could wear to school. All he could find was a pirate's hat that he'd worn in a class play in second grade. That wouldn't do the trick. It would just make everyone notice him even more. He thumped down the stairs.

Charlie came bounding down the stairs behind him. "Yo, Rob," he said, tossing his Yankees baseball cap to him as he passed by. "So long," he shouted as the door slammed after him.

Mrs. Dorfman shook her head as Robert entered the kitchen and grabbed a glass of orange juice. "I wish you boys would eat a decent breakfast before school."

Robert hardly heard what she said. He looked at the baseball cap. Charlie could be really nice sometimes. He put on the hat and ran out the door.

"Robert!" his mom shouted after him. But Robert was already on his way to meet Paul.

When they got to school, Robert left the cap on.

"Wouldn't you feel more comfortable taking off your cap, Robert?" asked Mrs. Bernthal.

"Um, no. I would rather wear it," said Robert. He slid down in his seat.

"Well, all right," said Mrs. Bernthal. "You may keep it on, if it means so much to you. I'm not a baseball fan myself, but I know how important it is to some of you."

"Yeah, right," said Matt. "Robert's a real sports fan." He giggled at his own joke. Everybody knew Robert was no athlete.

Except for Matt's remark, the rest of the morning went by without any teasing—until recess.

The boys were horsing around in the schoolyard. "Catch!" shouted Brian to Matt. Joey was in the middle, trying to get his hat back. As it sailed through the air toward Matt, Joey jumped up and caught it. Brian and Matt looked around for someone else to tease.

Before Robert knew it, Matt raced up and yanked his baseball cap off to continue the game. "Catch!" Matt shouted, tossing the cap to Brian.

Brian caught the cap and froze. "Look at Robert!"

"Holy cow!" said Matt.

"Robert! Where's your hair?" yelled Joey.

Robert had never felt so humiliated. The other kids gathered around to look at his hair—or what was left of it.

Paul came over. "It will grow back," he assured Robert. Good old Paul, to think of something thoughtful to say.

"Yeah," said Robert. He took the base-ball cap from Brian, who stood there with his mouth open.

It was absolutely amazing how naked Robert felt without his hair.

# Sunset Pines

"**C**lass, we're going to start a new project."

Robert, still wearing Charlie's baseball cap, sat up straight to listen. He could use something to take his mind off his hair.

"The Sunset Pines Senior Home needs volunteers to run small errands for some of the residents. Would you like to help?" said Mrs. Bernthal.

"Yes!" said Vanessa Nicolini and Emily Asher at the same time.

"Me, me!" said Susanne Lee, raising her hand. Other hands went up, including Robert's.

"What kind of errands?" asked Lester Willis. Lester never raised his hand. He just shouted out whatever he had to say.

"Oh, buying a box of tissues or a ball of yarn. Something like that."

Robert's hand was still up. Mrs. Bernthal stuck a piece of paper in it as she went around the room. "You'll need your parents' permission to go," she said. "Please have them sign this form." Robert tucked his permission slip in his notebook.

After dinner, Robert called Paul on the telephone. "Did your parents say it's O.K. to go to Sunset Pines?" he asked.

"Yes. My mom thinks it's a good idea to help the old people. Why?"

"I was just thinking. What if they send us on an errand to get something gross?" said Robert.

"Like what?" asked Paul.

"Like false-teeth cleaner," Robert said.

"Oh, yeah. Or corn pads. I guess we'll

just have to do it," said Paul. There was a pause. "As long as we don't have to try them out first."

Robert thought that was so funny he laughed until his sides hurt.

Friday finally came. At ten minutes of two, they left to board the school bus for the short trip to Sunset Pines. On the bus, Mrs. Bernthal reminded them of what they were to do.

"When you learn what your errand is, write it down," she said. Robert checked his pants pocket. He had a clean sheet of paper from his notebook, folded several times. A pencil was in his shirt pocket.

"You will have a week to do your errand. We will come back again next Friday," explained Mrs. Bernthal.

The nursing home had a big lobby. The walls were covered with pictures. Some were photographs of the residents at birthday parties. MRS. PITKIN, 90 YEARS OLD, read the label underneath one photo. Another said, JANE GREELEY'S 82ND BIRTHDAY. Mrs. Pitkin and Jane Greeley looked very cute in their party hats.

A woman in a bright pink suit came out to greet them. First she introduced herself to Mrs. Bernthal. Then she turned to the children.

"Hello, children. I'm Mrs. Mooney." Mrs. Mooney used her hands when she spoke. "I want to thank you for helping our residents with their errands. We are very grateful to you." She held her arms out wide, as though she wanted to hug them all.

"Come on," she said, motioning them to follow her. She led them to the lounge, where a TV set played. No one was watching it. There were people sitting around on sofas and in easy chairs. A few were in wheelchairs. Robert had never seen so many people in wheelchairs before.

"What's wrong with them?" he whispered to Paul.

Paul shrugged. "I don't know," he whispered back.

As they went around the room, Mrs. Mooney introduced the children to the elderly residents.

Robert was assigned to Mrs. Santini, a lady with crinkly white curls. She sat in one of the wheelchairs.

"Ah, a Yankees fan," she remarked, seeing Robert's baseball cap.

"Hi," said Robert. "I really don't know much about baseball. This is my brother's cap."

"I don't know much about baseball, either," said Mrs. Santini, "but Mr. Santini was a Yankees fan, so I went with him to see some games. We always had a good time. And I saw Babe Ruth play!"

Robert was impressed. He had heard of the great Babe Ruth.

For her errand, Mrs. Santini asked Robert to buy her some candy. She handed him a dollar.

"What kind of candy?" he asked.

"Not hard candy," she said. "That's for old ladies." She winked. "I want something you have to chew. I may not have all my own teeth, but I have some. And they feed us only soft food here. I need to chew something."

For some reason, that made Robert think of Trudy's chew stick. He had a terrible urge to laugh. He turned quickly to look out the window until he could control himself.

When the time was up, Mrs. Bernthal asked them to say good-bye and get back on the bus. Robert felt a little sad. The whole time he was with Mrs. Santini, he hadn't thought once about his horrible hair.

# Seven Wonders

"**W**ho was your old person?" asked Paul as they rode back to school.

"Mrs. Santini. Who was yours?"

"Mrs. Levine," said Paul.

"What did Mrs. Levine want you to get for her?"

"A magnifying glass," said Paul.

"A magnifying glass?" asked Robert. "Why?"

"She says she needs it to look up telephone numbers in her address book. Her eyesight is not so good."

"Oh," Robert said. "I never thought of that. Mrs. Santini wants me to bring her candy. Chewy candy." He smiled when he remembered what Mrs. Santini had said about the soft food at Sunset Pines and how he'd thought of Trudy's chew stick.

"What's so funny?" asked Paul.

Robert told him. They began to laugh.

"Maybe she'd like one," said Paul.

Robert couldn't hold it in anymore. They got sillier and sillier, holding their sides and laughing. It felt good to laugh, especially when you were nervous about something.

Robert had felt a little nervous being around all those people in wheelchairs. He felt sorry for them. He was also afraid, and he didn't know why.

"Do you think they are all sick?" he asked Paul.

"No. I think that when you get old, your legs just don't work so well anymore. It

happened to my gram. She uses a walker now. We see her all the time, and she comes over. When we go out and there's a lot of walking, she uses a wheelchair. But she's not sick."

That was good to hear. It made Robert wonder about Nana, his great-grandmother, who lived in Florida. She didn't visit them in River Edge anymore. Maybe that was why. It would be hard to travel with a walker or a wheelchair.

Robert knew exactly what to bring Mrs. Santini. He bought her a Seven Wonders bar. It had seven different ingredients—chocolate, caramel, marshmallow, coconut, walnuts, raisins, and cherries. It was pretty chewy.

"This is just the thing," said Mrs. Santini on their next visit. She put the Seven Wonders bar in her pocket and handed the change to Robert. "You keep that for yourself."

"Thanks," said Robert.

He sat down in the chair next to the window. "Do you have any errands for next time?"

"Well, you can bring me another Seven Wonders bar," said Mrs. Santini, reaching into her pocket. She fished out another dollar and handed it to Robert. "If it ain't broke, don't fix it," she said with a twinkle in her eye.

Robert didn't really understand what Mrs. Santini meant, and besides, he was wondering how come she used the word "ain't." Mrs. Bernthal told them "ain't" was like choosing a word from the bottom of the barrel, when they had such beautiful ones they could use from the top.

As the bus chugged along the streets toward school, Robert realized what Mrs. Santini had meant. "If it ain't broke, don't fix it" meant "If you like something the way it is, don't change it." He laughed out loud. That was a pretty good saying.

# Just Ask

After a few visits to Sunset Pines, Robert's hair had begun to grow in. He didn't feel so weird anymore. He stopped wearing the Yankees cap.

"Robert? Is that you?" Mrs. Santini said as he walked in one Friday afternoon in late October. "You look different."

Oh no! Not again. "Really? How?" he squeaked.

"I've never seen you without your baseball cap before," the old woman continued.

"Oh, that," said Robert. He smiled and

sat down. He pulled a Seven Wonders bar out of his jacket pocket and handed it to Mrs. Santini with her change. Again she made him keep the change. Robert thanked her.

"What did you think I meant?" asked Mrs. Santini.

Robert was glad to tell someone. "On the first day of school a girl in my class said I looked different." Mrs. Santini was listening very carefully. Robert continued, "I couldn't figure out what she meant. I thought my hair looked funny and I ended up with a terrible, horrible, no good, very bad haircut." He used the line from a book he'd once read about a boy named Alexander who had a "terrible, horrible, no good, very bad day." Robert smiled. He had loved that book. He wondered if Mrs. Santini would like to read it. "But I'm still not sure if that's what she meant," Robert finished.

"Why don't you ask her?" said Mrs. Santini.

*Ask her?* Robert stared at Mrs. Santini. He had never thought of that. Why not? The worst that could happen is that Susanne Lee would laugh in his face and humiliate him. But he was already humiliated.

That day, as he left Mrs. Santini, he had a big grin on his face. "See you next Friday!" he shouted. "And thanks!" He ran out to the bus.

"Susanne Lee!" he called. "Wait a minute!"

Susanne Lee spun around. "What?"

"I have to ask you something." Robert cleared his throat.

"O.K. Ask," said Susanne Lee.

"Remember what you said to me on the first day of school? About how I looked different?"

"Yes. So?"

"How?" asked Robert.

"How?" repeated Susanne Lee.

"Yes. How did I look different?"

Susanne Lee laughed out loud, just as Robert had expected she would. But it wasn't mean. "Robert, don't you know?" she said. "You must have had a growth spurt. You're so much taller. Can't you tell?"

"Um, no. I mean . . . sure. I . . . thanks. Thanks for telling me." Susanne Lee shrugged and got on the bus. Vanessa and Emily caught up to her, giggling.

Wow. Even with weird hair, Robert felt great. Imagine!  Being taller was the best back-to-school special of all!

# The Scariest Thing

The class trip to the Egypt exhibit was the best ever. Robert had nearly missed it. He kept forgetting to bring in his permission slip.

"Rob," his mom said, signing his slip on the morning of the trip, "do you think you could give me a little notice next time? You're lucky there was peanut butter and bread here so I could make you a sandwich." Mrs. Bernthal had called the night before to remind her Robert's slip wasn't in.

Robert had loved the whole exhibit, but the best part was the mummies. There was even a boy around his age who died thousands of years ago, and you could still see his face.

"Wouldn't it be the scariest thing if you were locked inside with the mummies after the museum closed?" Emily asked on the bus ride home.

Robert shuddered. That *would* be scary.

"The scariest thing for me was the time the lights went out in a storm," Andy Liskin said. "My mom sent me down to the basement for a box of candles. It was dark, and something ran by me. I thought it was a rat, but it was Puffball, our cat. She had followed me down the stairs."

"Oooooh." Abby shivered at the thought.

"I was watching a movie on TV once," added Vanessa. "It was really creepy. Just

when the scariest part came on, my cat jumped onto me from the bookcase. I didn't stop screaming until my mom threw cold water at my face."

Robert said, "My scariest time was when my brother hid in my closet and popped out to surprise me when I opened the door."

"You're all chickenhearted," said Matt. "I wouldn't be scared by any of those things."

"Yes, you would," said Andy.

"No, I wouldn't," said Matt. "I'm not a scaredy-cat."

"You should meet my dad," said Robert. "He can scare anyone."

"He can't scare me," Matt answered.

"Don't bet on it," said Paul. "You don't know Robert's dad."

Paul was telling the truth. He was at Robert's house often enough to know. Robert's dad was pretty normal most of the time, but just before Halloween, he changed.

He took out his horror collection. He watched videotapes of his favorite horror movies. He decorated the house with ghoulish delight. He loved getting ready for Halloween.

"Your dad sounds cool," said Brian. "You're lucky."

Robert had never thought of his dad as "cool" before. He had always thought of him as just a regular dad. But he did go ape over Halloween.

"So when do we meet him?" asked Emily.

"My dad?" Robert couldn't believe what he heard.

"Yeah," said Susanne Lee. "He sounds great." Wow. It took a lot to impress Susanne Lee.

"Well, Halloween is the best time. Come over to my house Saturday and see. I guarantee that he will scare you." Robert looked right at Matt when he said that.

As the bus drove up in front of the school, Susanne Lee, Vanessa, Emily, Abby, Brian, Matt, Andy, and Paul were talking about the Halloween party on Saturday at Robert's house.

# Surprise Party

"**A** party?" said Robert's mom. "Saturday?" She paced back and forth across the kitchen. Robert's dad was in the living room watching one of his videos. "Robert, you can't invite people to a party without asking me in advance."

"I didn't, exactly," said Robert. "I just said that Dad could scare anyone, even Matt Blakey, and they should come over and see him for themselves around Halloween. The rest just sort of happened."

"What's this?" asked Robert's dad. He had clicked off the video and come into the kitchen.

Robert explained. His dad looked pleased, but Robert's mom was still pacing. "The house is a mess," she said. "I have a bridal shower to go to on Saturday and I won't even be around."

"I will," said Robert's dad.

"Yeah, Mom. Dad and I can do it." Robert thought it would be great to have the party with just his dad home. His dad wasn't as strict about things as his mom.

"Right," said his dad. "What do we have to do?"

"Well," she sputtered. "Cleaning . . . and you'll need party treats and paper goods and . . . and . . . decorations . . . and . . . entertainment . . ."

"We can do all that, Clare," said Robert's dad. "Don't worry." He winked at Robert.

"We'll go shopping together after school tomorrow."

Robert looked at his dad with a big thank-you in his eyes.

Robert's mom gave in. She said she would tidy up the house if they did the rest.

"Let's get the stuff from the basement and see what we've got," said Robert.

Mr. Dorfman was a real movie fan, especially horror movies. He had a collection of costumes, masks, props like fake hands and scars, theatrical makeup, and other stuff. He even had a Dracula cape he once wore to a grownup party at a horror fans' convention. Every Halloween, the collection came out, and Robert found things he had forgotten about since last year.

Robert's dad went down to the basement and brought up a big cardboard box marked "HORROR." He went back for two more cartons after that.

They opened the cartons in the living room. In one were the rubber masks and hands. Next came the makeup case, the Dracula cape, and various props. In the third box were assorted decorations.

"Look, here's Henry," said Robert. He unfolded a huge skeleton with movable limbs. "Can I hang him?" he asked.

"Sure, Tiger. Go ahead."

Robert opened the front door and hung Henry right next to the door knocker. The hook was still there from last year.

Digging into the box again, Robert pulled out cardboard pictures of horrible creatures. He taped them to the front windows to look like they were peering out.

Next came bloody hands, bloodshot eyeballs, fake guts, bats with flapping wings, phony cobwebs, and various electronic items, like talking boxes and dismembered hands that walked across the table when the batteries were turned on.

Last, but not least, was the Halloween tree. Every year they set it up and hung creepy ornaments on its branches. Robert smiled. Halloween at the Dorfman house had begun.

# Too Late Now

On Friday, Robert was ready when his dad got home from work. He raced outside and jumped into the backseat, hooking his seat belt.

"Can we go to the party store first?" he asked.

"O.K., we'll start there," said his dad.

They bought party games and prizes, decorations, paper plates and cups and napkins, and miscellaneous spooky figures and toys. One was a witch who cackled and whose eyes flashed red when you lifted her up.

Robert felt a little weird. He knew his mom would have made him put half the stuff back by now, but his dad just let him keep adding to the cart.

Next, they went to the Super Shopper. As they stood in line at the checkout, Robert began to worry.

"Dad, is Charlie going to be at my party?"

"Your brother was invited to a party at Barney's house," his dad answered. That was a relief. Charlie could be a real tease and spoil things.

They waited while the clerk rang up three packages of disposable diapers for the person ahead of them.

"What about music, Dad? And entertainment?"

"Got it under control, Tiger. Will you stop worrying? This is going to be fun."

"Dad?"

"Yes, Robert?" The line moved up by one person, and they started putting their bags of candy and jugs of juice drinks on the moving belt.

"Will you tell some of your scary stories? Please?"

"Sure, if you want me to," answered his father. "I think you're worrying too much. You'll have a great party. I have a few surprises in mind guaranteed to send kids screaming." He grinned.

Robert smiled back. What was his dad going to do? Would his friends like being scared or would they think his dad was weird? Halloween was sort of about being scared, so he hoped they would like his dad's surprises. Sometimes they could be

pretty surprising, but that's what was such fun. Would the other kids see it that way? Maybe he should have just gone out trick-or-treating.

The cash register rang out *ching! ching! ching!* It was too late now to change his mind.

# Uncle Albert

**R**obert got out of bed and staggered into the bathroom. He got dressed, fed his birds, Flo and Billie, and said good morning to Fuzzy, his tarantula. She moved her legs slightly, which was her way of saying good morning.

He thumped downstairs, and as he brushed aside the fake cobwebs hanging in the kitchen doorway, he remembered: It was Saturday—the day of the Halloween party.

Last night, he had stayed up late putting up pictures of witches and skulls and black cats. On the coffee table, the crystal polar bear had been replaced by the plastic witch with the glowing eyes. Robert lifted it up to hear the witchy voice cackle.

His dad must have stayed up really late. He had hung the cobwebs and draped all the furniture with black crepe paper streamers. The Halloween tree stood on the dining room table, all assembled with bats and worms and spiders hanging from its branches.

Robert sat at the table and poured Crispy Crunchy Flakes into a bowl. He reached for the milk container and poured. It was green.

"Mo—o—m . . ."

"It's your father, dear." His mom sighed. "He put food dye in the milk. It's harmless."

He should have known. Robert smiled. "Where is Dad?" he asked, spooning in some of the cereal.

"In the living room. But finish your breakfast first."

Robert gulped down his cereal and washed it down with orange juice.

He found his father stuffing an old plaid flannel shirt and a pair of jeans with newspapers.

"What are you doing?" Robert asked.

"Getting Uncle Albert ready," said his father. He lifted the stuffed clothing onto the easy chair in the corner. Robert watched as his dad tucked the shirt part into the pants part. Then he stuffed socks with more newspaper, stuck them inside a pair of his shoes, and added these to the rest of the figure in the chair. Without the head and hands, it looked something like a scarecrow, but a lot scarier.

Robert's dad picked up an over-the-head rubber mask of a bald guy with bushy eyebrows and a deep frown on his face. The lower lip hung a little. The face was wickedly ugly. Robert's dad stuffed more newspaper inside the mask.

"Here, help me with this, Tiger," he said. Robert opened the neck of Uncle Albert's shirt while his dad put the mask in place. Where the neck of the mask met the shirt, his dad tied a scarf around and knotted it.

"What about his hands?" asked Robert.

"I'm glad you asked," said his dad. He lifted up two big hollow rubber hands, all gnarled and hairy. He arranged them so they stuck out of the shirt cuffs. Uncle Albert looked natural and relaxed, his hands resting on the arms of the chair and his legs crossed. It was perfect.

As Mrs. Dorfman walked through the living room, she did a double take. "Oh

my," she said. "He looks so real, sitting there."

"That's the point," said Mr. Dorfman. Robert saw that his dad was having fun.

"I can't wait for the kids to see Uncle Albert," said Robert.

"Do you think Matt Blakey will like it?" his dad asked.

"I'm sure he'll like it," Robert said, "but I don't know if it will scare him. He says he's not scared of anything."

"Ah, a challenge," said his dad. His eyes gleamed. "I love challenges."

"How are you going to scare him?" Robert knew his dad well enough to know he'd been thinking up ideas.

"You'll have to wait to find out, Tiger. I can't spoil all the surprises for you. You already know about Uncle Albert."

# Vel-l-l-l-come!

**R**obert decided to get into his costume so his mom could see him before she left for the bridal shower. At first, he was going to be a monster, wearing the rubber mask his dad had given him. Then, after he saw the Dracula cape, he changed his mind. His mom helped him put on the theatrical makeup—green on his skin, black around his eyes, dark shadows on his cheeks to make them look sunken, and bright red lips. A set of vampire teeth made it perfect.

"You're the best vampire I've ever seen,"

she told him as she snapped a picture for him to show Mrs. Santini next Friday.

Having his mom around, Robert felt everything was going to be O.K. When Robert saw her blue Toyota leave the driveway a few minutes later, he felt a little less certain.

The doorbell rang around five o'clock. Robert leaped from the sofa and ran to the door. Emily came in first, in a witch costume with a tall, pointy hat. Brian followed her as a Martian.

"Vel-l-l-l-come," Robert the Vampire said. He held his hands high and clawlike, spreading open the cape.

Mr. Dorfman, in his over-the-head were-wolf mask and a pair of hairy hands, pointed the way into the living room. The children saw Uncle Albert and stopped short.

"Come right in," said Mr. Dorfman. "This is Uncle Albert. He doesn't say much. He just likes to . . . observe." Emily and Brian hung back.

Next came Vanessa as a ballerina, Matt as a mad doctor in a white lab coat with red stains all over it, and Paul in a clown suit with a big red rubber nose.

"Meet Uncle Albert," said Robert's dad to the new group. "He's not very sociable." The kids stared, but only Matt moved closer. He went up to the dummy's face and looked into its eyes. Vanessa squealed. When Matt was convinced it was just a dummy, he moved away from Uncle Albert and into the dining room. The table had been set up with the Halloween tree and bowls full of miniature candy bars, orange and black jelly beans, marshmallow ghosts and black licorice cats, candy pumpkins and candy corn.

"Help yourselves," said Robert. He tried not to sound too cheerful. After all, he was a vampire. He grabbed a handful of black and orange jelly beans for himself. Matt left to take another look at Uncle Albert. This time he poked a finger into Uncle Albert's chest. After a little more poking, he left the dummy alone.

More kids arrived. Susanne Lee came as the Statue of Liberty, Abby as a cat, and Andy as a mummy, with toilet paper bandages wound around him and trailing behind. Robert introduced them to Uncle Albert. Susanne Lee walked right up to him and said, "Oh, hello, Uncle Albert." When she turned around, she jumped. Mr. Dorfman's werewolf mask got her. Robert had to laugh.

Robert's dad kept the music playing. Sometimes he played eerie background music from horror movies, and sometimes the sound of witches cackling, creaky doors, and howling winds. Robert recognized these from a special effects CD that his dad owned.

Matt still looked suspiciously at Uncle Albert. Finally, he joined the rest of the kids as they were getting ready to bob for apples in the kitchen. Matt was plenty curious, but he didn't seem the least bit scared.

# Eyeballs and Worms

**R**obert's dad, no longer in his werewolf mask, had a huge covered pot in his arms. "Who's hungry?" he called.

"What is it? What is it?" the children cried.

"My own special stew," said Mr. Dorfman with a devilish grin. "I need someone—a brave soul—who will put his hand into this stew of mine and stir it around."

"No way," said Brian.

"Uh-uh, not me," said Paul. The boys laughed nervously, but nobody moved.

The girls all stayed frozen in a huddle.

"Ah," said Mr. Dorfman. "Is everyone afraid, then?" He turned to Matt. "You, Matt. Are you afraid?"

Matt stepped forward. "I . . . I'm not afraid. What's in there?" he asked.

Mr. Dorfman blindfolded Matt. "Only eyeballs and worms," he said. "It won't harm you."

"Eee-yew!" said Abby, backing away. Emily hid behind her. Robert smiled. He knew it was just peeled grapes and cold spaghetti, but he didn't tell. Mr. Dorfman took the lid off the pot and guided Matt's hand to the edge of it.

"Reach in, real deep," said Mr. Dorfman. Matt put his hand farther into the pot. "Yuck!" he said, making a horrible face.

"Now fish around until you find a card. Pull it out and read it. You have to do whatever it says."

Matt pulled his hand out, waving a card.
He removed his blindfold.

"What does it say?" asked Paul.

Matt read, "Hop around the room on one
foot while crowing COCK-A-DOODLE-DOO."

As the children watched, Matt started hopping and crowing. Giggles and howls filled the room.

"I'll go next," said Susanne Lee. She did, and everyone watched for signs that she was getting grossed out. She was fine. Her card read, recite "Mary Had a Little Lamb" backward. Paul went next. He had to do a somersault.

The games continued for a while. They were playing pin the tail on the black cat when the doorbell rang. It was the pizza delivery guy.

Mr. Dorfman invited the children into the dining room. He put two pizza boxes on the table. Brian eagerly opened one box and yelled in surprise. It was filled with rubber snakes. The second box revealed a bloody finger, fake guts, bloodshot eyeballs, a dismembered ear, and a piece of brain.

"Eee-yew!" cried Vanessa, but she giggled.

"Gross," said Emily, in spite of the smile on her face. Matt just smiled

Mr. Dorfman exchanged the two boxes of horrible things for two other boxes, this time real pizza. "Help yourselves," he said, and they all dove for a piece.

# Scary Stories

**R**obert had just bitten into a piece of pepperoni pizza when his dad walked back in. "Would you like me to tell a scary story?" he asked.

"Yes!" they all cried.

He turned out the lights, lit a single candle that cast weird shadows on his face, and began to spin a spooky tale.

It was about creaks in the floor and a corpse rising from the grave and bodies buried in the walls of a house. The children were spellbound. When Mr. Dorfman

finished one story, they asked for another.
He told a gruesome story about a floating
head that came bobbing down the stairs at
night, its eyes aglow.

With each addition of something more horrid or loathsome, there were groans and gasps and whimpers.

As the story ended, the candle went out, and they were in the dark. Robert had seen his dad do this before. He kept very quiet. Without warning, Mr. Dorfman let out a scream, and they heard and felt a thud. The children jumped up, screaming, in the dark. Mrs. Dorfman came running in, still in her coat, and turned on the light.

"Mom," said Robert. "You're home."

Mr. Dorfman was stretched out on the floor. He opened his eyes. "Hello, Clare," he said.

"I think maybe that's enough fright for one Halloween night," she said.

"Oh, please, Mrs. Dorfman. We won't scream anymore. Honest." The children begged for more, but Mrs. Dorfman was firm.

"Maybe next year," Mr. Dorfman told them. He winked.

"It's time for cake," said Mrs. Dorfman. "Take your places at the table." The children went back to their seats.

As they dug their plastic forks into the cake, frosted in orange icing, Mrs. Dorfman poured a cherry-colored fruit drink into their paper cups.

Robert went up to his father. "Dad, you haven't scared Matt Blakey," he whispered with some urgency.

Mr. Dorfman frowned. "I know. You were right. He's a really tough case."

# Gotcha!

"**R**obert, why don't you take your friends up to your room to see your tarantula?" said Robert's mom.

Robert stared at his mom. Sometimes she could surprise him. She had never showed any interest in his tarantula before.

"O.K." he said. "Follow me."

"You have a tarantula?" said Brian, his eyes wide.

"That's a spider, right?" asked Emily in a shaky voice.

"Yes, a huge spider," said Robert, hoping that would scare Matt a little.

Upstairs in his room, Robert introduced them to Fuzzy. He told them how he got her when Susanne Lee brought her over one day because her cat wanted to eat Fuzzy.

"Everybody knows Robert loves animals," Susanne Lee said. "He seemed like the right person to adopt Fuzzy."

Robert did not add that Susanne Lee had practically forced the tarantula on him. Or how scared he was to sleep in the same room with Fuzzy at first.

After the children saw Fuzzy and Robert's doves, Flo and Billie, they went back downstairs. Mrs. Dorfman reminded them that it was almost eight o'clock, so they should begin to gather their belongings. "Your parents will be here soon," she said.

They sat around the living room, clutching their bags of treats. They no longer paid attention to the figure in the easy chair, except for Matt. He went over and reached out to touch Uncle Albert's sleeve. Suddenly, the figure grabbed him. Matt let out a scream so loud the rest of the children

started screaming as well. Mrs. Dorfman came running. Vanessa was hiccuping between screams. Abby ran for the bathroom and locked herself in.

Mrs. Dorfman went over to Matt and put her arm around his shoulders. "It's only a trick," she said, comforting him. Uncle Albert stood up. The children were transfixed. Matt clung to Mrs. Dorfman.

Meanwhile, Robert talked to Abby through the bathroom door to convince her it was O.K. to come out. "It was only a trick, Abby. Come on, you'll see." Abby came out, but she stayed very close to Robert.

"This is our neighbor, Tom," said Mr. Dorfman, pointing to Uncle Albert. "He agreed to come over to help with the surprise." Tom took off the hands and the Uncle Albert mask.

"Hi," he said.

"You . . . you were in there . . . the . . . the . . . whole time?" Matt stammered.

"No," said Mr. Dorfman, "While you were upstairs, Tom made the switch, getting into Uncle Albert's clothes. I put the mask and rubber hands on him and got him into the same position the dummy had been in."

"Robert, you were right," said Susanne Lee. "Your dad is fun!"

"Yeah," said Matt. "This was a great party."

"Thanks," said Robert, catching his dad's eye.

As parents arrived and thanked the Dorfmans, Robert overheard some of the conversations.

"It was great!" Brian told his mom.

Susanne Lee told her mom the scary stuff was "awesome."

Vanessa told her dad the best part was listening to scary stories by candlelight.

When Matt's dad picked him up, he said to Matt, "So, did you have a good time?"

Matt nodded. "Dad, I was so scared, I jumped ten feet!" They went off toward their car, Matt chattering away.

In the house, Robert looked at his dad. His dad looked at him. As they closed the door behind them, they gave each other a high-five.

# The Stranger

Everyone but Paul had been picked up. He was staying overnight with Robert. They were tired but a little wound up, so the two boys lounged on the sofa while Mr. Dorfman tidied up the living room around them. Robert picked up the plastic witch and listened to her cackle. Her eyes glowed on and off. He and Paul giggled.

In the dining room, Mrs. Dorfman was clearing off the table, dumping paper plates and used napkins and forks into a big black trash bag. Robert was glad his mom was home in time for some of the party, anyway. Even though she didn't let them carry on with their tricks as much as his dad did, it felt good to know she was there.

Paul got up to help clear the table with Mrs. Dorfman. Robert followed.

"Well, thank you," said Mrs. Dorfman. "I never had a vampire and a clown help me with the cleanup before." They smiled, too tired to answer.

At last, they said good night and climbed the stairs to Robert's room. They got out of their costumes and scrubbed off the makeup.

"Don't you wish sometimes you could be as surprised as everyone else by your dad?" asked Paul.

Robert thought about it. "No, it's O.K. I kind of like being in on the jokes and watching other people see them for the first time."

"Did you know about Uncle Albert and Tom?"

"I suspected it, but I didn't know for sure until my mom sent us upstairs. I knew they needed us out of the way for something, and that was probably it."

As they got into bed, they heard a noise out back, in the yard. Robert got up and went to the window. He motioned for Paul to come, too.

Paul gasped when he looked down. Below the window was an ugly stranger in a trench coat. The stranger stared up at them.

"See what I mean?" said Robert. "That's my dad again. That's another mask he's wearing. We'll pretend to be scared, but I know it's him."

Robert pretended to scream and threw his hands up in the air. Paul followed him and did the same, jumping around like he was really frightened. While they were at the window, acting scared, there was a knock on Robert's door.

Robert went to the door and opened it. There stood his dad.

"AAAAAAAH!" Robert screamed. Paul screamed. Robert ran to the window. The stranger was still in the yard, so it couldn't be his dad!

"Dad! Look!" Robert went back to his dad and pulled him to the window by his sleeve.

Mr. Dorfman looked out the window.

"See him?" Robert asked.

Mr. Dorfman nodded. "I'll go down and see who it is," he said. "You stay here."

Robert and Paul watched nervously from the window as Mr. Dorfman appeared in the yard and approached the stranger. The stranger held up his fists as if he wanted to fight.

"Look out, Dad!" Robert called.

Both men looked up at the window . . . and waved, as Tom, the neighbor, pulled off his rubber mask.

"Oh no!" said Robert.

"They got us!" said Paul

"Yeah," said Robert. "He even fooled me." His dad really *was* cool.

The boys fell back into bed, collapsing in laughter.

"Paul?" said Robert, after they turned out the light.

"Yeah?"

"Next year I'm going to have a party and invite the whole class."

"But your mom said you can't invite kids over for a party without asking her."

"No, she said I can't invite people to a party without asking her *in advance*," said Robert. "This time I'm asking her a whole year in advance."

He pulled the covers up over his head and went to sleep.